Boris

E.J.Chambers

To Mark x Sue
Watch out for
Tray Trolls!
EJ Chambers

DEDICATION

To the staff and pupils of The Cathedral Catholic
Primary School.

ACKNOWLEDGMENTS

A big thank you to the very talented David Accialini for his wonderful pictures that have brought Boris and his friends to life and to the children and staff at The Cathedral Catholic Primary School for their constant naggings to actually put my stories down on paper.

CHAPTER 1:
SYBIL

Have you ever wanted something really badly? I mean REALLY badly, so badly that you can't think of anything else. Sybil had and today it had caused her all sorts of trouble. In fact, it was the reason that she was now lying on her bed, in her room, having been sent up with no tea and told not to come down until she was prepared to apologise.

It's just not fair, she thought. *I mean, all I said was I wanted a pet dragon! Is that really so bad?*

Of course, that was not all that Sybil had said. In fact, the discussion had been a lot longer and a lot louder than that and had started with the phone call from Mrs Higham, Sybil's class teacher.

The day had begun well. It was Friday and that meant pizza for school dinner and art in the afternoon. Sybil had skipped to school whistling tunes from the school play and thinking about how she could spend the weekend.

English had been fun. They were writing stories about fantasy worlds and Mrs Higham had said they could create their own characters and write anything they wanted about them as long as it included all the capital letters and full stops, had interesting words and some connectives in and was in joined up handwriting. Sybil wasn't sure if her story contained those things. However, it did have a mystical portal, a brave princess called Sybil and, of course, a huge and fearsome dragon. What did a few capital letters matter after all? As long as there was a dragon in the story!

You have probably gathered by

now that Sybil liked dragons. In fact, they were the thing that Sybil spent most of her time thinking about. She longed for a dragon of her own. It would be big and scary with glowing red eyes, shining purple scales, sharp teeth and razor-like talons. It would breathe fire and would be called something like Fang or Razor, but most importantly, it would stop Lisa Massey, who sat next to her in class, from laughing at her all the time. I mean, no one is going to laugh at you if you have a pet dragon, are they?

Sybil did not like Lisa Massey. She was one of those girls who never seemed to do anything wrong. She had long, curly blonde hair, beautiful blue eyes and cute dimples in her cheeks. Sybil had short brown hair, mucky brown eyes and could never be called cute. Lisa always got all her work right and Mrs Higham gave her lots of house points for her beautiful presentation and handwriting. Sybil spent a lot of her playtimes sat in the classroom rewriting work that was considered too scruffy and untidy. However, the worst thing of all as far as Sybil was concerned was that Lisa Massey always seemed to be laughing at her. When Sybil got an answer wrong in class, Lisa laughed. When Sybil had to stay in at playtime, Lisa laughed and when Mark Porter put a spider in Sybil's tray and made Sybil scream, Lisa laughed so much she nearly fell off her chair. No, Sybil did not like Lisa Massey at all and that was where the trouble had started.

"Today we are going to make a bar chart of our favourite pets," Mrs Higham had announced. "Can anyone suggest which pets should be on our list?"

Mark Porter had put his hand up and suggested dogs. Mrs Higham had said that was a very good idea and put it on the list. She had said the same when Lucy Smith had suggested cats and

Tracey Devitt had said hamsters. Sybil put her hand up as high as she could so Mrs Higham would pick her.

"Sybil, I will not pick you if you wave at me and make strange exploding noises!" said an exasperated sounding Mrs Higham. Lisa Massey laughed. Sybil tried to sit sensibly.

"That's better Sybil. Now what animal do you think we should add?"

"Dragons, Miss," Sybil shouted enthusiastically.

"Sybil! If you can't make a sensible suggestion then don't say anything at all. We are not in the infants!"

"But I am being sensible, Miss. I want a pet dragon!"

"Sybil! Dragons are not real and I really think we need to move on with the lesson."

"But...."

"Not now Sybil!"

Lisa Massey turned and grinned at Sybil.

"Baby," she whispered, so Mrs Higham couldn't hear. "Only babies believe in dragons."

"Miss, Lisa called me a baby!"

Mrs Higham just sighed and turned to Toby Edwards for another animal suggestion. Lisa Massey smirked at Sybil and Sybil imagined her being eaten by a giant, fire-breathing dragon.

* * *

Sybil was late to lunch; apparently, capital letters and full stops were important in stories. Even ones with mystical portals and cool dragons. By the time she got to the front of the dinner queue there was no pizza left, just fish fingers. Lisa had got the last piece of pizza and stood grinning at Sybil from across the canteen.

"Baby..." She mouthed at Sybil and then turned to her friends. They all laughed.

That was the last straw. Sybil stormed across the canteen and pulled Lisa's long, blonde hair.

Mrs Taylor, the head teacher, had been very cross with Sybil and when Sybil had tried to explain, Mrs Taylor wouldn't listen, especially when Sybil started to tell her about Maths and the dragons.

"Sybil, you are in Year 4 now. You need to start taking responsibility for your own actions. Dragons are for infants."

Sybil was not allowed to do art

that afternoon, instead she had to write a letter of apology to Lisa. Her eyes stung as she fought back the tears, but she wasn't going to give Lisa the satisfaction of seeing her cry. She would only call her a baby again. Instead, she thought about her dragon and all the amazing adventures they would have together.

The afternoon seemed to last forever, but eventually the bell rang and Sybil escaped school for the day. As she walked home, she started to feel more cheerful. The sun was shining and she had the whole weekend to look forward to but her brighter mood was not to last long.

She had been home about fifteen minutes when the phone rang. Dad talked to Mrs Higham for a long time. All Sybil could here were comments like "Oh dear…" "I see…" and "We will talk to her…" When the phone call finished, the row started. Sybil couldn't remember exactly what she had said but it had ended with her being sent to her room and told not to come down until she would apologise and that there was to be no more talk of dragons.

Sybil lay down on the bed and stared at the celling. She was never going to go back downstairs and she would certainly not stop thinking about dragons. She knew they were real, even if no one else would believe her!

CHAPTER 2:
BORIS

It was still dark when Sybil woke up. She was cold and hungry and was beginning to think that being stubborn and staying in her room rather than going downstairs and apologising had been a very bad idea. She was not a naughty girl and didn't like making her parents cross and she certainly didn't like missing her tea! In fact, it had been her tummy rumbling that had woken her up!

"I didn't know your tummy could rumble so loudly you could hear it in your sleep," she mumbled to herself as she pulled off her jeans, put on her pyjamas and crawled under her duvet to get warm. (She had cried so hard the night before that she had fallen asleep on top of her bed and no one had come to tuck her in.)

Sybil was just starting to settle back down to sleep when she heard it again.

"Grrr….."

It sounded like her tummy but it definitely wasn't coming from her! Nervously, Sybil sat up. She pulled her torch from under her pillow and started to move the small beam of light slowly around her room.

"Grrrr…..hick…..bother!"

Sybil tried to point the torch to where the sound had come from, but her hands were shaking so much that she dropped it. She didn't want to get out of bed to put the light on so she sat in the dark and listened, hoping that tiredness and hunger were making her hear things.

She waited quietly in the dark room feeling as if her heart would burst out of her chest because it was beating so quickly. *It sounds like someone playing the drums,* she thought. *If there is something in here, surely it can hear me*? However, there was no movement and no more strange sounds. Gradually Sybil began to relax, and thought that perhaps she might be brave enough just to reach down to the floor by her bed and pick up the torch. She didn't think it would have rolled too far on the carpet and the light would help her just check the room one more time before she went back to sleep. As quietly as she could, she started to stretch out her arm.

"Grrrrr…..Hick…..Bother! Bother! Bother!"

This time the noise was accompanied by a strange burning smell and a glow coming from the end of Sybil's bed!

Sybil flew out of bed to the light switch as fast as her legs would carry her.

"Who's there?"

"What do you want?"

"Oh…"

As the light filled the room, Sybil's eyes were met with the strangest sight she had ever seen…

There, sitting on the end of her bed, trying to cover the singed patch on the duvet with its tail was a small, pink, fluffy dragon. Yes, I did say, "dragon," and I did say, "pink and fluffy." You can understand why Sybil was so amazed.

Slowly, Sybil walked towards the dragon. She was not afraid. After all, this was what she had wished for. Ok, perhaps not quite what she had wished for, there were no razor-sharp claws, red eyes or shiny scales, but at least it was a dragon. Now everyone would have to believe her when she said that dragons were real. She had proof, it was sitting on her bed and apparently it had the hiccups!

"Are you just going to stand there with your mouth open or are you going to help me?" exclaimed the hiccupping dragon in a rather exasperated kind of voice.

"Don't you know that a dragon with hiccups can easily burn a house down?"

"Really?" said Sybil.

"Well what should I do then?"

"Pick me up and rub the middle of my back. That usually works."

Sybil didn't need asking twice. The dragon looked so soft and fluffy and it really was rather cute. She scooped it up into her arms and gently rubbed its back. It made a strange rumbling noise, which she could have sworn, was a purr, but surely dragons didn't purr? Mind you, half an hour ago she hadn't thought they could be pink and fluffy either.

Slowly, the dragon stopped hiccupping. No more unexpected flames came from its mouth and it settled down in Sybil's arms.

"I like you," it said. "I think I might stay here."

"Oh, that would be great!" exclaimed Sybil, with a big grin on her face. "I always wanted a pet dragon. Can I call you Fang or maybe Razor?"

"Pet! Pet! I am nobody's pet, thank you very much! And no, you can't call me Fang or any other silly name. I will have you know young lady that I am one hundred and two years old and my name is Boris and I am not and never have been anybody's pet!"

"I am so sorry," whispered Sybil in an apologetic tone. "I didn't mean to offend you."

"That's alright. Just don't do it again. I will probably forgive you if you rub my back some more and perhaps tickle me behind my ears. Dragons like that."

Sybil sat on the end of her bed with Boris on her knee not quite able to believe what she was hearing. She tickled the dragon gently behind his ears and he settled back down rumbling contentedly.

"Where did you come from?" Sybil eventually asked.

"Here and There," Boris replied. "I just knew that tonight it had to be Here. It's kind of complicated."

"I can't wait till you meet everyone. They think dragons aren't real and now they can't say I'm being silly anymore."

"I'm afraid that can't happen," said Boris quietly. "You see, you are the only one who can see me. To everyone else I am invisible unless it is really, really important"

"It *is* important!"

Sybil thought she might burst with frustration. The most amazing thing had happened. Something she had always wanted and she couldn't tell anyone. One thing was for sure, though, life was never going to be quite the same again. How could it be? She had a real, live dragon living in her bedroom. How cool was that? Even if she was the only person who could see him.

CHAPTER 3:
BORIS AND THE BULLY

The rest of the weekend seemed to fly past. Sybil spent most of it in her bedroom playing with Boris and tickling him behind his ears. He wasn't a fussy eater and she had been carefully smuggling up scraps from the table for him after each meal. To avoid any more hiccups she made sure that she gave his back a good rub after each meal and so far there had been no more fiery accidents.

She had turned her duvet over so that her mum did not see the singed patch and opened the window to get rid of the burning smell. The only real disappointment of the weekend had been the discovery that Boris only seemed to be able to breathe fire when he had the hiccups. Apparently only big, scaly, scary dragons can breathe fire when they want to. Small, pink, fluffy dragons can only produce the occasional accidental spark.

Sybil's parents had a good weekend too. Sybil had come down stairs on Saturday morning in a much better mood and had apologised for her outburst the night before. They did notice that she seemed to be spending more time than usual in her bedroom and they had occasionally thought that they had heard her talking to herself but there had been no more talk of dragons and that was good enough for them.

Sunday evening came around too soon as far as Sybil was

concerned. As she was getting ready for bed, she grumbled to Boris, "I wish I never had to go back to school ever again!"

"Why?" asked Boris looking rather puzzled.

Sybil told Boris all about the event of Friday morning and in particular the row with Lisa Massey. "I am fed up with her laughing at me all the time. It makes me feel all funny in my tummy. I get really cross and shout at her and that just makes her laugh at me more!"

"Well perhaps we need to do something about it," Boris replied thoughtfully. "I will come to school with you tomorrow."

"How will that help if no one can see you?" complained Sybil.

"You just leave that to me."

With that promise still going round in her head Sybil went to sleep feeling better than she had about Mondays for a very long time.

The bell rang on Monday morning and all the children ran to their lines. Boris had come to school with Sybil, just as he had promised. She wanted to laugh as she lined up. It was hard not to with a fluffy dragon sat on her shoulder tickling her ear.

"What are you grinning about, Baby?" sneered Lisa, from behind her in the line.

"Is that her?" asked Boris.

"Yes," sighed Sybil.

"What did you say?" said Lisa.

"Errr nothing," stammered Sybil.

"First dragons, now talking to

herself. There's no hope," said Lisa to her friends and they all turned away and laughed.

Sybil wanted to cry, but she looked at Boris, who suddenly had a very fierce look in his eyes and the smile slowly crept back to her face.

Sybil's first job that morning was to apologise to Mrs Higham for her behaviour the preceding Friday. She had promised her parents that she would and although she still didn't feel that the incident had been all her fault she knew that sometimes the best course of action was to take a deep breath and move on. She could feel Lisa's eyes on her back as she went to Mrs Higham's desk to say sorry and she really hoped Mrs Higham would be too busy to make a big deal out of it, but she was out of luck.

"I should think you are sorry young lady. That is not the kind of behaviour we expect in this school. I hope we are going to have a better week, this week!"

"Yes Miss," Sybil muttered and scurried back to her desk before Mrs Higham could give her one of her many lectures about taking responsibility for her own actions.

As she crossed the classroom she could see the smirk forming on Lisa Massey's face, and sat down waiting for the unkind comment that she knew would follow the smirk. She didn't have to wait long.

"So you're a creep now as well as a baby are you? Sorry Mrs Higham, I won't do it again Mrs Higham," Lisa mimicked in a squeaky, babyish voice.

Sybil was about to open her mouth to retaliate when Boris put a soft paw on her hand and whispered.

"Leave this to me."

By this time, Boris had moved from Sybil's shoulder to sit on her lap. This was much better as far as Sybil was concerned because when he was on her shoulder the fur on his tail tickled her neck and made her want to giggle. She absent-mindedly tickled him behind his ear and started to feel a little better, although she had no idea how an invisible dragon could help solve her problems if no one could see or hear him.

Sybil suddenly realised that Lisa Massey was watching her as she stroked Boris. Lisa put her hand up and whispered, "You're for it now, Baby."

"Yes, Lisa?" asked Mrs Higham, with a smile on her face that she never used when she spoke to Sybil.

"Mrs Higham, Sybil has a toy on her knee," Lisa said in her sweetest voice, the one that the teachers seemed to love and made Sybil feel sick.

"Really..." Mrs Higham replied

as the smile left her face.

She walked across the classroom to the desk Sybil shared with Lisa and looked down at the two girls. A puzzled look crossed her face.

"I thought you said Sybil had a toy in school, Lisa?"

"She does, Miss. It's on her knee. It's a toy dragon"

Mrs Higham looked carefully at Sybil and Boris smiled up at her and waved.

"I think you must be mistaken,

Lisa. There is nothing on Sybil's knee. Now I think we need to get on with our lessons."

"But it's right there!" exclaimed Lisa.

As she said this, Boris turned towards Lisa and slowly stuck his tongue out at her.

"Miss… She just made that toy pull a rude face at me!" Lisa shouted. "It must have batteries or something, because it keeps moving!"

As if on cue, Boris stood up and started moving from Sybil's knee towards Lisa. Sybil struggled to keep the smile from her face as Lisa squirmed in her chair and let out a squeal.

"Lisa Massey, sit still!" shouted Mrs Higham.

"But the dragon moved again, Miss."

"There is no dragon, Lisa. I can only assume that this performance is designed to try and get Sybil into trouble. I am surprised at you. Now, do I need to ask you to leave the classroom?"

"N-no, Miss."

Lisa looked as if she might cry. She was not used to being in trouble and she could clearly see the pink dragon sat on Sybil's knee. She couldn't understand why Mrs Higham couldn't. Perhaps she was imagining things or feeling unwell. She looked across at Sybil again. It was still there, sat on her knee, pulling faces. Sybil could see the confusion in the bully's eyes and almost felt sorry for her.

"I thought no-one could see you?" she whispered to Boris.

"I told you, no-one can see me unless it is important… That was important!"

Sybil looked at Lisa and smiled sweetly at her. Boris looked at Lisa and pulled the rudest face he could manage. Lisa started to open her mouth, thought better of it and tried to get on with her work.

At break time, Sybil popped Boris back on her shoulder before she went out to play. It was the first playtime she could remember in ages when Lisa and her friends had not made fun of her. In fact, some of the girls that usually played with Lisa came to play with her instead. Lisa stayed as far from

Sybil as she could and, when they went back into class, she asked Mrs Higham if she could possibly move to a seat at the front of the classroom so she could see the board better. Mrs Higham agreed and put Tracey Devitt next to Sybil instead.

"I like dragons," Tracey whispered as she sat down, "and you are okay too."

Sybil smiled down at Boris. *I always knew a dragon would sort Lisa out*, she thought, even though a small part of her still wished that it was a big scary one that could breathe fire.

CHAPTER 4:
BORIS AND THE MISSING PENCILS

Why did it always have to happen to her? Sybil thought as she frantically searched through her tray for her pencil. It felt like every morning Mrs Higham asked them to get their pencils out, Sybil opened the tray under her desk and hers had gone… again… She knew just how this was going to end. She wouldn't be able to find the pencil. Mrs Higham would stand at the front waiting for her to be ready. She would have to admit that she had lost her pencil… again… and she would get one of Mrs Higham's lectures about the fact that pencils don't grow on trees, that equipment costs money and if the class budget gets spent on replacing things people don't look after, there is nothing left for the nice things.

Oh well, better get it over with. "Mrs Higham, I can't find my pencil."

"Sybil… pencils don't grow on trees you know…"

Sybil had to stay in at break time and write out 'I must look after school equipment' fifty times.

"It's not fair!" she grumbled to Boris as she scrawled out the sentences. "I know I put my pencil in there every night, so what's happening to it?"

Boris looked thoughtful. Then he bent down and sniffed at Sybil's tray, which Sybil thought was most peculiar, and a little bit revolting.

"I think I might stay here tonight

and do a bit of investigating," he said. "I like a good mystery and I think I may just know what's happening." However, he wouldn't say any more, no matter how much Sybil asked.

When the bell went that evening, Sybil carefully put her pencil at the front of her tray next to her pen and ruler. *Funny how neither of them ever go missing,* she thought. Then she closed her tray and gave Boris a quick hug.

"Are you sure you will be alright here on your own?" she asked him.

"Of course I will. I'm a dragon. We are used to spending time on our own in dark and dangerous places!"

"What about classrooms?" Sybil laughed.

"I am sure I will cope, just save me some cake for breakfast tomorrow."

"Will do," said Sybil and she set off for home.

It felt strange going home without Boris, but Tracey was coming for tea that night and Mum had promised cake so Sybil was sure that she wouldn't miss him too much. She headed off to the playground to meet up with Tracey. Since Boris had sorted Lisa Massey out, Tracey had spent quite a bit of time with Sybil and the two girls had become firm friends.

Left alone in the classroom, Boris sat on Sybil's desk and waited. He watched as Mrs Higham went around the room sorting out the classroom after the day's lessons. He even went and sat on her desk while she was marking books. He was very tempted to hide her red pen when she got to

Sybil's book, but he knew he couldn't interfere and after over one hundred years of helping unhappy children, he had also realised that Mrs Higham was actually right and capital letters were important.

At five o'clock, Mrs Higham packed the remaining books into her bag and went home. Mr Williams, the school caretaker, came into the room grumbling about untidy children and teachers, hoovered the floor and cleaned the desks ready for the next day. Boris still sat and watched.

Eventually the school emptied and night began to fall.

Now, thought Boris, we *will see if my theory is correct.*

The school hadn't been in darkness more than half an hour when Boris heard the first noises.

"Get yer fat foot out of my face!"

"You get yer face off me foot, then!"

"Will you two pack it in or I will bash both of yer 'eads together!"

"You'll 'ave to get 'is off me foot

first…"

This conversation was followed by loud laughter and large amounts of banging and clattering. It was all coming from Sybil's tray.

The tray started to rattle and move and, as Boris watched, it slid open before the owners of the voices started to climb out.

"I thought as much," muttered Boris and kept watching.

"'Ere look, lads, that batty teacher of theirs 'as got another one of them stupid puppets."

"It looks like a dragon to me, but who ever saw a pink dragon!"

"I told ya, she's nutty as a fruit cake that teacher of theirs!"

"I think yer might be right Sid. 'Ang on a minute lads, look what I found!"

"What is it Fred?"

"A new battle stick, I'll be king of the tray with this!"

As Boris watched a tiny, ancient-looking man crawled from the tray to join his two companions, and in one very gnarled-looking hand he held Sybil's new pencil. The three little creatures danced around the table top in glee, holding the new pencil high in the air.

The racket had obviously drawn attention to the small group, as soon, other little creatures started to crawl out of the mess of crumpled paper and odd gloves that made up the contents of Sybil's tray. Several of them were holding pencils, all of differing lengths and ages. The little men all stood in a ring on the table top waving their pencils excitedly.

"Tray Trolls," Boris muttered. "Just as I thought, but what could they possibly want with all those pencils?"

Boris was soon to find out the answer as a chant went up from the assembled tray trolls.

"Fight, fight, fight, fight…"

The troll, who Boris had previously worked out was called Fred, was stood in the middle of the table waving Sybil's new pencil over his head.

"Come on yer cowards, I challenge yer to come and let me

bash yer daft 'eads with me new battle stick!"

Another, slightly younger looking troll stepped forward to accept the challenge, and soon the two trolls were hitting each other over the head as hard as they could with the pencils.

Boris had seen enough.

"Stop!" he bellowed as loudly as he could and flew over to the table, landing in the middle of the ring and scattering tray trolls across its surface.

"Blimey! It's not a puppet after

all!"

"No… but I still think pink is a stupid colour for a dragon."

At that, Boris shook his head and muttered something under his breath. Then he addressed the little people in front of him. The negotiations that followed lasted late into the night and it was nearly dawn by the time an exhausted but satisfied Boris curled up to go to sleep on the bean bags in the book corner. As he dozed off, he smiled and felt very grateful that he was only invisible to humans, not other magical creatures.

Sybil skipped happily into class the next morning and smiled as she opened her tray to see her pencil lying exactly where she had left it. As she went to take it out for Maths, a small piece of paper fell out onto her lap. She opened it and read:

DEER SYBIL

SORY WE GOT YU IN TRUBLE WIV YER TEECHER.

WE WILL YOOS THE PRITTY BATTUL STICKS WOT BORIS GIVED US IN FEWTUR.

THE TRAY TROLLS.

P.S. PLEEZ CAN YER BRING US SUM CAKE

Sybil read the note twice and then looked at Boris.

"It's a long story," he yawned. "I just hope nobody needs the old coloured pencils from the spare pencil tray any time soon."

With that, he curled up on Sybil's lap and went to sleep. Sybil looked down at her new best friend and smiled.

It's a good job no one can hear him snoring, she thought and carried on with her Maths.

ABOUT THE AUTHOR

E.J.Chambers is a primary school teacher from
Lancashire in the United Kingdom.
She constantly has to replace pencils which have been
used by battling Tray Trolls and has an invisible (not
imaginary) classroom dragon called Boris who assists in
the prevention of the pilfering of stationery.
She is also the long-suffering wife of urban fantasy and
horror author A.S.Chambers.

Printed in Great Britain
by Amazon

69279288R10043